It's Just a Stage

Also available in the Road to Avonlea Series

It's Just a Stage

Storybook written by

Amy Jo Cooper

Based on the Sullivan Films Production
written by Marlene Matthews
adapted from the novels of

Lucy Maud Montgomery

HarperCollins*Publishers*Ltd

IT'S JUST A STAGE
Storybook written by Amy Jo Cooper

Copyright © 1992 by HarperCollins Publishers Ltd,
Sullivan Films Distribution Inc., and
Ruth Macdonald and David Macdonald

Based on the Sullivan Films Production produced by Sullivan Films Inc.
in association with CBC and the Disney Channel with the participation of Tele-
film Canada adapted from Lucy Maud Montgomery's novels.

Road to Avonlea is the trademark of Sullivan Films Inc.

Teleplay written by Marlene Matthews
Copyright © 1990 by Sullivan Films Distribution Inc.

Canadian Cataloguing in Publication Data
Cooper, Amy Jo
It's just a stage
(Road to Avonlea ; 19)
Based on the Sullivan Films Production adapted from the novels of
Lucy Maud Montgomery
ISBN 0-00-647389-X

I. Title. II. Series.

PS8555.O56I87 1992   jC813'.54   C92-094624-0
PZ7.C66I87 1992

Design by Andrew Smith Graphics Inc.
92 93 94 95 96 ❖ OFF 10 9 8 7 6 5 4 3 2 1

Chapter One

"I betcha he won't," Felix insisted stubbornly, more because his older sister seemed so snooty about being right than because he really cared.

Felicity rolled her eyes and pursed her lips with a knowing superiority. "He always does."

"Well, maybe he won't this time."

"Some things," Felicity said, with a manner almost prophetic, "never change."

Felix King knew better than to argue. He held his tongue and trudged sulkily behind Felicity as they made their way through the crowds at the Winter Fair. Colorful banners flapped in the breeze, bringing a touch of warmth and gaiety to the dull November sky.

They wound their way through the muddy fairgrounds, Felix hanging his head until they reached the pen where the livestock was judged. Felix pushed through the crowd gathered for the judging and climbed onto the bottom rail of the old fence, hoping to get a better view. He scraped some of the mud that clung to his boots onto the splintery, gray wood and waited.

The Avonlea Winter Fair was an annual event. Folks came from all over the Island bringing their vegetables, their preserves and pickles, their baked goods and their livestock, all to be judged, auctioned and prized. It was the biggest event to occur in Avonlea between summer and Christmas, so naturally, everyone was excited.

For weeks before the fair, everyone in Avonlea contemplated, debated and discussed who would have the prize heifer, who would win the ribbon for her pies. Every category was thoroughly considered and disputed, from quilting to quarter horses. Every category, that is, except pigs. When it came to pigs, there was never a surprise.

Theodora Dixon picked her way across the puddles carefully in an attempt to keep her freshly polished boots away from the mud. The boots had seen better days, and although worn, they had been mended and tended in a well-intentioned, if perhaps a bit haphazard fashion.

The late-autumn sky dripped gray as Theodora, fists clenched tight, heart fluttering, scurried through the milling crowd. She knew she'd have to hurry if she wanted to be in time for the judges' announcement of the winning pig. More than a few heads turned as Theodora took her place at the livestock pen, but she was more intent on the swine within than the people without.

"First prize for the best pig at the Avonlea Winter Fair ..." Mr. Biggins stopped and looked around. He hoped, with his pause, to generate some excitement, a little suspense, but, in this case, he knew it was a lost cause.

"The first prize ..." Mr. Biggins repeated, looking around at the crowd, who seemed only mildly interested in the outcome. A few people murmured their impatience; one man coughed. Mr. Biggins gave up. No use stalling any longer. With a note of resignation, he continued, "... goes to Pat Frewen and his pig Lulubelle."

"See, what did I tell you?" Felicity smirked,

looking like the cat that swallowed the canary. "Some things just never change."

Felix leaned his chin on the top rail of the fence and refused to answer her. For the last twenty-odd years, which was as far back as most people could remember, Pat Frewen had always owned the prize-winning pig.

"Oh, Pat! Oh, Pat!" Theodora squeaked, breathless with excitement. "I knew you'd win." She seemed to be the only one truly surprised.

Pat Frewen looked briefly in Theodora's direction before accepting his ribbon from Mr. Biggins.

To see Pat's sow take the prize was not the reason most people gathered at the livestock pen. The real show was to be found in the on-going drama between Pat and Theodora Dixon. For twenty years, Theodora had been bent on becoming Pat Frewen's wife. But Pat was not an easy catch. Folks gathered at the pigpen each year as much to see whether Theodora had snagged him yet as to see his pig take the blue ribbon.

"Congratulations, Mr. Frewen." Mr. Biggins beamed as he pumped Pat's hand. "Fine-looking pig you got there."

Pat Frewen grunted his thanks and took the ribbon. Then he lumbered towards the exit of the pen dragging a reluctant Lulubelle, who clearly would have preferred to stay and bask further in her glory.

No sooner was Pat out the gate than Theodora anxiously accosted him.

"Pat? Pat, you said you would come over for tea after the fair. We could celebrate Lulubelle's win. I made butter tarts."

"Lulubelle don't like butter tarts, Theodora. You know that."

Confused and slightly flustered, Theodora replied, "No, the butter tarts are for you, Pat."

Poor Theodora, Felicity thought as she eyed the eager spinster trying so hard to win the man she loved. Everyone said that Pat was just too stingy to marry her. Given how she cooked for him three nights a week, how well she took care of him, how devoted she was, Pat had all the advantages of marriage without paying a thing.

Poor Theodora! Felicity sighed again. Some things truly never change, she mused to herself as she and Felix threaded their way through the festive crowd.

The clattering of horses' hooves shook Felicity

from her reverie. The buggy from the White Sands Hotel was rattling along Avonlea's main street, its roof laden with baggage.

"It's her!" Felicity screeched, grabbing Felix's arm and nearly scaring him out of his wits. "It's Pigeon Plumtree!"

Pigeon Plumtree, the famous actress, renowned for her beauty, her mellifluous voice and her tragic flair, had come, after many years' absence, back to Avonlea. The purpose of her visit was not thespian but personal. She wanted to see the child of her beloved cousin, Blair Stanley. She had heard that twelve-year-old Sara had grown into a remarkable child, both beautiful and full of wit. Pigeon, childless herself, had a great desire to make the acquaintance of this dear girl, and to lavish on her the affection she would have lavished on her own sweet daughter, had fate ruled otherwise.

The buggy turned the corner sharply on its way to the hotel. A small valise tumbled from its mountain of baggage and landed indecorously in the mud. The driver halted the vehicle.

"Somebody kindly pick up my valise," a deep, rich voice ordered imperiously from within. Before the sentence was finished, Pat Frewen, moving faster than anyone had ever seen, had scrambled over to the wayward luggage, scooped it up and offered it to the person inside.

"Miss Plumtree," Pat stammered, "welcome back. I remember the first time I saw you perform in Charlottetown, twenty years ago."

A white-gloved hand reached out of the window and retrieved the case. "Thank you, my good man. Now, goodbye. Driver, to the White Sands Hotel."

Then, as quickly as it had arrived, the buggy departed. Pat Frewen stood as still as a statue watching it depart.

Behind him, a forlorn Theodora, her bright hopes flickering, heaved a mournful sigh. "Oh Pat."

Chapter Two

Rose Cottage was all in a flurry. Each of its inhabitants scurried hither and thither, checking on this, polishing that. Everything must be right. A visitor was expected—an important visitor!

Sara had been floating on cloud nine ever since Miss Plumtree's daintily perfumed letter arrived. To think that Pigeon Plumtree was coming here, to Avonlea, to see her! The thought was so divine, so uplifting that Sara's feet had barely touched the ground for weeks.

Sara had often heard about her father's cousin, but she had never met her. Pigeon Plumtree spent most of her time touring around the world, performing in all the famous theaters. She had even performed before the Crowned Heads of Europe. There was a family story, whispered mostly among the adults, of a prince who had fallen madly in love with Pigeon and had pursued her through Europe, but Sara wasn't sure of the details.

Sara polished the silver serving spoon until it shone like a mirror. The whole table sparkled and glistened. She had convinced Aunt Hetty to use the good china—the white with the rose pattern—and, after much entreaty, their best crystal glasses, the ones her father had sent all the way from Ireland. She checked her reflection in the handle of the spoon, then placed it back down on the snowy-white damask tablecloth.

A story formed in her mind, a story of fame and glamour. Sara Stanley, world-famous actress, stands on the stage, having just performed the best Juliet the world has ever seen. Her arms are laden with roses, and more flowers rain down, thrown by her adoring fans. Nodding modestly, she humbly takes her bows to a standing ovation and shouts of *Bravo!*

Then, at a sumptuous dinner party given in her honor at a castle somewhere on the Rhine, the beautiful Sara Stanley, resplendent in her gown of wine-red velvet, chats wittily and charmingly to some of the Crown Heads of Europe.

Later that evening, on a parapet overlooking the sweeping river below, a dashing young prince declares his love. The moon glints off the many medals pinned to the blue of his tunic. His sabre, sheathed at his side, clatters against the cold, gray stone of the castle as he drops to his knee. His fine black mustache tickles as he presses his lips fervently to the back of her dainty, gloved hand.

"But no, Prince," she tells him gently, "as much as I care for you, my first love is —" and here, she pauses dramatically, "— the Theater."

"Now don't you dawdle, Sara Stanley, there's work to be done." Aunt Hetty's voice burst through the bubble of her imagination. In a flash, the prince, the castle, the admiration faded like ghosts at the first light of dawn. In their place, Sara saw her pretty Aunt Olivia mashing the potatoes and her Aunt Hetty, a crisp white apron tied firmly around her waist, icing a chocolate cake.

Hetty King was not a flighty woman. Nor did she care for such frivolity as the theater or other such brouhaha. She was not going to all this fuss because some world-famous actress had decided—with precious little warning—to drop in out of nowhere, just because she had some whimsical notion to see her cousin's daughter— the very child that she, Hetty King, had been raising. No, the King family had their pride, and Hetty had the greater portion of it. She would entertain Pigeon Plumtree in the finest style because she was Sara's family.

"The Stanleys have always put on airs," Hetty complained silently to herself. "Who do they think they are? Just because they've traipsed all over the world and not stayed put like sensible people, they think they know better than anyone. Well, I'm not going to have this, this flibbertigibbet looking down her nose at me!"

Hetty was in a fine snit now. She squeezed so hard on the pastry bag that the last of the icing spurted out and landed on the cake with a loud *splat*.

Hetty looked up to see the inquiring eyes of Olivia and Sara. She collected herself. "It's not the Queen coming to dinner, you know, Sara. Miss Plumtree is just a plain, ordinary woman."

"But she isn't a plain, ordinary woman," Sara protested, "she's a world-famous actress."

With a quick wave of her hand, Hetty dismissed the notion. "Well, I have no time for actresses. They're just vain, useless creatures."

"Hetty, acting is a noble profession," Olivia sweetly interposed. Her pink cheeks deepened to an even pinker shade, as they always did when she chose to contradict her imperious older sister. "You make the children at school recite poetry all the time. That's acting."

Hetty bristled at her sister's good sense. "Reciting poetry isn't acting. It's memory work." Hetty never liked to be corrected, especially when the other person might be right. "Oh, it's completely different. Actors—actors are deceivers. People who pretend to be someone else for a living aren't right in the head, if you ask me."

An impatient knock at the door stopped Olivia from responding to her sister.

"Oh dear," Hetty whispered, as flustered as a schoolgirl waiting for her beau, "she's here."

No one moved. Then everyone moved at once. "Stay calm," Hetty ordered, "I'll get it." Hetty straightened her hair and quickly removed her apron, then headed for the door.

Sara and Olivia were glued to their spots, frozen with anticipation. The moment Sara had been waiting for had finally arrived. She was almost ready to explode with excitement.

Chapter Three

Another loud, impatient knock sounded on the door. Goodness, Hetty thought to herself, does the woman have no manners? Determined to teach Miss Plumtree a thing or two about patience, Hetty paused before the door, intending to wait a few seconds before she let her in.

But just then, the door burst open, spilling Felicity and Felix into the room. Aunt Hetty had just enough time to hop out of the way before being bowled over.

"Heavens!" she managed to squeak.

"Sara," Felicity shrieked, her eyes bright with excitement, "we've seen her!"

"She's here!" Felix chimed in, caught up in his sister's enthusiasm.

"We've seen her," Felicity repeated. "We've seen your cousin, Miss Plumtree. We saw her buggy."

From the moment she had laid eyes on Pigeon Plumtree, Felicity couldn't wait to tell Sara. She knew her cousin would just die when she found out that she had seen Miss Plumtree first. But now that she was there, the desire to irk her cousin disappeared in the whirlwind of her exhilaration.

"Oh Sara, she's utterly magnificent! Her hat was ..." Felicity searched for the right word,"... gorgeous! Oh, and her cape, her cape was just ..." But the proper adjective escaped her, for in all her thirteen years Felicity had never seen a cape as wonderful as the one Pigeon Plumtree wore.

Sara grabbed her cousin's hands. "Don't leave out a word," she beseeched her. "I'm all goosebumps."

Felix jumped in before his sister could respond. He hadn't really seen Miss Plumtree herself, but he had seen her luggage, and her gloved hand extended out the window of the buggy. This, he supposed, made him almost as great an authority as his sister.

"She must be filthy rich. She had suitcases piled to the sky. Everyone in town was staring," Felix added.

"Felix King," Aunt Hetty admonished, having almost recovered from the shock caused by the sudden appearance of her niece and nephew. "*Filthy* properly applies to the condition of a room, or a person, to denote their respective states of uncleanliness, physical or moral. To apply it to a person's economic status is slang. And I will not have slang spoken in my house."

"Yes'm." Felix hung his head. Why was he the one who always got bawled out? It wasn't fair, he decided, swiftly kicking the leg of a nearby chair, then quickly and guiltily looking up in case anyone had noticed.

But everyone was too caught up in the particulars of Pigeon Plumtree to have seen his transgression. Sara stood rapt with attention, devouring every word. Aunt Olivia, too, listened eagerly, clutching her dimpled white hands in front of her as if in prayer. Even Hetty was curious.

Felicity's vocabulary was stretched to the limit to describe Miss Plumtree's traveling outfit. Unfortunately, it wasn't in her power to provide enough detail to satisfy Sara.

"I didn't see her close up. I only saw her as the carriage passed by," Felicity was forced to admit. "I don't know if it was an ostrich feather on her hat or not."

"Vanity," Hetty muttered, with a superior smirk.

"Oh, but Sara, I do know that she was beautiful beyond words, and I can't believe she's coming here for dinner!"

As if on cue, Sara and Felicity both gave little squeals, then jumped and danced around in their delight.

"Children, children," Hetty reminded them over the ruckus, "she is not the Queen. She is just an ordinary person."

Chapter Four

Plumtree, of course, was not her real name. She had been born a Stanley. Plumtree was the stage name she had adopted at the beginning of her career. "Pigeon Stanley" fell flat upon the ear, far too prosaic to encompass her prodigious talent. "Pigeon Plumtree" rolled

trippingly off the tongue in a far more satisfy-
ing way.

Pigeon checked her appearance in the mirror.
Deftly, she twisted her thick, sandy blond hair
into a fat roll and pinned it up. Then, just to add
to what nature had already given her, she
painted just a touch of lip rouge on her Cupid's
bow lips. She smiled at her reflection, pleased
with what she saw. If her beauty had not the
freshness of her youth, it had, at least, ripened
into a fine handsomeness.

Pigeon put on her traveling hat and adjusted
the ostrich feather. Then, with a quick pat, she
coaxed back her chin, which had lately started to
droop.

Pigeon did not seem to walk so much as float
across the rose-patterned carpet in the lobby of
the White Sands Hotel. The gray silk of her skirt
rustled slightly as she progressed. All heads
turned and all eyes watched her. But Pigeon
walked straight ahead, seemingly unaware of the
admiration. Only the slight, self-satisfied smile
that played on her lips betrayed her pleasure.

"I shall need a carriage," she informed the
flustered desk clerk.

Olivia pulled back the white sheer curtain one more time and peered down the road. Still no sign of Miss Plumtree. Then, with a great sigh of disappointment, she let the curtain drop back to its place. She was almost an hour late. The family at Rose Cottage had gone past impatience all the way to extreme fidgeting.

"Oh, Aunt Hetty, this table is never going to do," Sara exclaimed as she rearranged the candles for the fourteenth time.

"For heaven's sake, Sara," Hetty snapped, her nerves frayed, "leave that table alone."

Felicity dropped the silver serving spoon she was polishing, then hastily picked it up. "Can you see the buggy yet, Aunt Olivia?"

"No, not yet."

In three swift strides, Hetty was by Felicity's side. She plucked the now dirty spoon from her niece's hand before she could place it back on the table.

"Felicity, Felix, go home," Hetty ordered, holding her niece firmly by the arm.

"But Aunt Hetty, I just want to see what she's wearing. Can't we wait?"

"I don't want the two of you standing around gawking as if you've never seen a dress before.

Now, run along. Both of you."

"I promise I'll take careful note of every stitch she's wearing," Sara vowed to Felicity, whose woeful look touched her deeply.

"I don't care what she's wearing," Felix called over his shoulder as he was being firmly escorted to the door. "Just save me a piece of cake."

"Here comes the buggy," Olivia shouted, sending everyone into a dither. "Quick, light the candles."

Everybody moved at once, going hither and thither with no one going any place in particular.

"Where are the matches?" Sara demanded, rifling madly through the drawers.

Felicity ducked out from under Hetty's grip and grabbed the matches from the mantelpiece. "Here they are," she called triumphantly as she handed them to Sara.

Hetty paced back and forth, fretting and fussing. She stopped for a minute and absent-mindedly wrung her hands. "Such a fuss over nothing," Hetty stewed, but, she too was nervous. "Sara, careful, you'll burn the house down. Olivia, Olivia, move the pots, move the pots."

There was a knock at the door. All motion

stopped. Where there had been chaos, there was now complete and utter stillness.

"*I'll get it*," they all shouted at once. Then, in a crush, everyone scrambled together, pushing and jostling as each tried to be the first to the door.

"I'm mistress of this house," Hetty commanded. "I'll get it."

Everybody stood at attention as Hetty, marshaling her forces, thrust out her chin, squared her shoulders and opened the door.

Chapter Five

Pigeon Plumtree sailed into the entry hall on a cloud of roses and lavender. As she swept in with one great turn, her cape—dove gray, made of fine French wool crepe—swirled and fluttered grandly around her, exposing its scarlet silk lining. It was a magnificent entrance.

Sara was enthralled. Never before had she seen a creature so glorious, so divine. She marveled at Pigeon's beauty. She had a fine, round chin, a short, straight nose and plump, pretty red lips. Her complexion made Sara think of snow and roses. Her large dark eyes were expressive and, Sara imagined, could as easily flash with anger or melt with sorrow.

Everyone gawked at her in fascination. Pigeon looked round from center stage and gave a disarming smile for the benefit of her admirers. She possessed a commanding appearance and, although not a large woman, her presence seemed to overwhelm the room.

Hetty was the first to recover her voice. "Ah, uh, Miss Plumbush—uh, tree—Plumtree," she hastily corrected herself. "I'm Hetty King. I'm Sara's aunt. The one who has been taking care of her these last few years." Hetty's smile was a tight line across her face. She wanted Miss Plumtree to know who was in authority here.

Pigeon met Hetty's stare with an equally level gaze. She smiled at her sweetly. The two women would have stared at each other forever, each determined to get the upper hand, if Felicity had not broken the silence by clearing her throat.

Hetty regained her composure and remembered her duties as hostess. Gesturing towards her niece and nephew, she added, "Oh, and this is Felicity and Felix King, Sara's cousins."

Felicity managed to drop a pretty curtsey. She had one handy that she always practiced, in case she ever met royalty. Felix just stood there staring, his mouth wide open, his lower lip dangling.

Hetty gripped first Felix, then Felicity, firmly by the shoulders. "They were just leaving," she said, escorting them to the door.

"Darlings, darlings, darlings, must you leave so soon? The evening has just begun." Pigeon's voice was deep, the tones rich. The words did not so much fly from her throat as roll from it.

Both Felix and Felicity looked longingly at their aunt, hoping against hope that Hetty might be persuaded. But once Hetty had made up her mind there was no changing it. She ushered them onto the veranda. With a delicate shove, Pigeon closed the door behind them.

Hetty was a bit surprised and even more annoyed to find herself outside on the porch with the door shut behind her. "The nerve of that woman," she muttered as she reached for the doorknob.

Sara waited expectantly. Her heart pounded so loudly she was afraid that Pigeon would hear. Oh, what if she doesn't like me? she worried. All of a sudden, Sara regretted her choice of dress. Although it was one of her best—blue muslin, French cut—it seemed somehow drab. If only

Aunt Hetty had let her put up her long, blond hair instead of wearing it with a ribbon, like a child! She felt awkward and provincial before such worldly manners and cosmopolitan flair. Sara wished that the floor would open up and swallow her whole.

"Now which of you two adorable girls is my cousin Sara? Let me see." Pigeon first turned her gaze on Olivia, who blushed and timidly lowered her head. Then Pigeon's eyes landed on Sara and sparkled with joy. "You, I'd know you anywhere. You shine like a beacon in the night."

Pigeon dashed the cape from her shoulders. Hetty entered the house just in time to catch the expensive garment before it crumpled to the floor.

Pigeon grandly motioned for an embrace, her graceful arms extending widely as if to encompass the world. "Dear heart," her fruity tones beseeched, "come, dear child. Come kiss cousin Pidgey-poo."

As Sara ran into her cousin's embrace, all her fears disappeared and her greatest hopes were realized.

"Pidgey-poo?" Hetty muttered, her eyebrow arching almost to her hairline. "Well, I never ..." she muttered sourly as she watched the elaborate display of affection.

Pigeon held her niece out at arms' length and regarded her fondly. Sara, remembering her manners, sweetly spoke what she had been rehearsing for weeks. "It's nice to meet you, Miss Plumtree."

Pigeon gave Sara's shoulders a gentle shake. "Sara, darling, stop right there," she admonished. "Stop right there. We are family, dearest. You must call me Pigeon."

It had been her secret wish, and it had come true. She was on a first-name basis with Pigeon Plumtree, the world-famous actress.

The table looked perfect as they entered the dining room. The silver gleamed, the crystal sparkled, the candles glowed. Sara felt no small pride at their efforts and hoped Pigeon would be pleased with their offering.

"Oh, how quaint," Pigeon cooed, "you've made a little snack."

"Snack?" Olivia exclaimed, perhaps a bit rudely. But then, she did find Miss Plumtree's remark to be somewhat ill-mannered. "We've been cooking for two days."

"Oh, what a shame. I have a very delicate stomach. Diverticulitis, you know. Little bumps in the stomach lining, very tender. I rarely eat. I have vertigo as well," she cheerfully informed them. "It makes me quite bilious if I look at food."

Sara's heart sank with disappointment. How silly of her not to realize that an artist with as finely tuned a temperament as Pigeon's would naturally be physically fragile. She wished to offer her something, at least a small token of her esteem.

"Well, Miss Plumtree—I mean, Pigeon—won't you sit down and have some tea, perhaps?"

"Tea? I'm sorry, darling, tea upsets my nerves." Pigeon noted the disappointment on Sara's face. "However, I could manage a small fizz, with just a nip of gin and some seltzer water. For medicinal purposes, of course."

Hetty sniffed. "We don't partake of spirits in this house."

Pigeon regarded her and smiled. "No, I don't imagine you would. Perhaps you have a little something sweet we could eat?"

"We have a chocolate cake," Olivia offered, pleased that something could be salvaged. "My sister Hetty made it. She makes the best chocolate cake in Avonlea. The whole Island, in fact."

"Pshaw, Olivia," Hetty demurred, outwardly modest but secretly pleased.

"Cake? No, I'm afraid, my loves, that it would be too heavy. Much, much too heavy."

"How about those imported chocolates that we're saving, Aunt Hetty?" Sara asked.

"Absolutely not," Hetty snapped. "They're a King tradition. They mustn't be opened till Christmas."

Pigeon's features looked remotely peeved. Her gracious smile only slightly masked her displeasure. Her attitude gave one the impression that she had somewhere else she would rather be.

Sara's hopes were dashed. If they didn't offer her something, she was afraid Pigeon would leave. There was an anxious moment of silence. Sara racked her brain, desperately trying to think of something to offer their guest.

"We do have some elderberry wine," Olivia suggested hopefully, for she, too, felt it a shame not to be able to offer something.

Pigeon brightened. She flashed a brilliant smile. Sara basked in its light. "A glass of wine. Yes, that will settle my dizzy spells."

"I know exactly where it is." Sara raced off, delighted to be of service.

Chapter Six

With a little peck here and a little pick there, Pigeon managed, in spite of her delicate stomach condition, to swallow more than a few morsels of food. In fact, she made quite a respectable meal, which she cheerfully washed down with several glasses of elderberry wine.

"Some more wine, Miss Plumtree?" Hetty asked sourly.

"Oh, darling, I couldn't," Pigeon announced, at the same time reaching for the decanter and pouring just a splash more into her glass. "But, if you insist ..." She smiled, very graciously, as if she were doing Hetty a favor.

She does quite well for herself, Hetty thought, for someone who has difficulty eating.

Hetty watched as Olivia carefully edged the mashed potatoes in Pigeon's direction. Without pausing in her conversation or looking at the serving dish, Pigeon reached for the spoon and helped herself to a second serving. Hetty and Olivia pretended not to see. It was as if they had silently agreed to act in a charade.

If there was any falseness in Pigeon, Sara did not notice. So captivated was she by Pigeon's stories of the theater and the theatrical life that the vivid pictures they evoked were all she saw. Pigeon's rich, mellifluous voice conjured up images of all the great stages of London, Paris and Rome. Sara was transported. Gone the table, gone Rose Cottage, gone the sleepy little town of Avonlea. In their place, Sara felt the heat of the footlights and heard the thunderous roar of applause. Pigeon's ability to create illusion knew no bounds.

Pigeon charmed both Sara and Olivia with her tales of the theater. She beguiled them with stories of great performances she had seen thrilled them with a yarn of an ill-fated production of *Macbeth*; amused them with anecdotes about fussy stage managers and vain leading men who would stop at nothing to upstage every actor in the play.

Pigeon acted every part, her voice now deep and resonant, now soft and lilting. Only Hetty was not enchanted. To her, it was just plain poppycock.

The candles were all but burnt down. It had been a wonderful evening, surpassing all of Sara's expectations.

"You'll have to move closer to me, darling." Pigeon clasped Sara's hand and drew her near.

"You know, the more I look at you, the more I see your dear departed father ... the eyes, the nose ... definitely." Pigeon addressed Olivia and Hetty. "Sara looks exactly like our Great Aunt Eugenie."

"I do?"

"Right down to the fingernails. You know, Great Aunt Eugenie was not only a spectacular beauty but an actress of great renown. Acting is very much a family tradition."

"Along with diverticulitis and vertigo, I have no doubt," Hetty muttered.

"Hush," Olivia admonished, but her soft brown eyes sparkled with mirth.

Sara's heart leapt with excitement. "A family tradition? Really? Oh, Pigeon, it has always been my greatest dream to be an actress."

"Since when?" Hetty inquired sharply. "Last week it was a singer. Before that it was a writer."

Sara wanted to object. Perhaps she had never come right out and stated her wish to act, but she knew in her heart that it was so. Unfortunately, the objection had no chance to materialize, for Hetty had more to say on the subject.

"Acting," she said with great distaste. "It can hardly be said that acting develops the mind."

"*Au contraire*, Miss King. Acting is excellent training for the mind," Pigeon countered, with only a touch of haughtiness in her tone. "Why, I can recite all of Shakespeare's plays by memory. I've played all the most important leading ladies, you know, in the course of my illustrious career."

"I certainly don't intend that Sara become a leading lady of anything," Hetty declared. Only Olivia nodded with her in agreement, for Sara was too excited to notice.

"Pigeon, I adore *Romeo and Juliet*. Do you think that one day I could play Juliet?"

"It is part of your heritage, dear heart. It is in your blood."

"It is?"

"Perhaps you could come visit me after school tomorrow at the White Sands Hotel. We could get better acquainted."

Pigeon rose from the table, signaling that the evening was at an end. Olivia hastily rushed into the entry hall. She quickly returned carrying Pigeon's cape, hat and gloves. Suitably attired, Pigeon strutted grandly into the front hall. Perhaps the elderberry wine was to blame for a slight unsteadiness in her otherwise elegant gait.

"Goodness," she said, smiling sweetly at Hetty, "I've drunk so much my back teeth are floating." She closed her eyes and furrowed her lovely brow. Placing her fingertips delicately on her temple, she declared, "I do feel a crushing headache coming on. However," and here she opened her eyes and looked directly at her young cousin, "Sara darling, I believe you mentioned something about imported chocolates. Chocolate is very good for headaches, if I remember correctly."

Sara looked hesitantly at her Aunt Hetty, caught between her desires and duty.

"Go on, Sara," Hetty said reluctantly. She was too worn out from the evening to argue any further. "Give her the chocolates. I certainly wouldn't want to have her headaches on my conscience, too."

After sampling a few of the divine confections so happily offered her, Pigeon graciously accepted the whole box of chocolates imported all the way from Belgium. Then, with a flourish, she exited.

Thus, the evening ended. But, as with all good performances, memories of it lingered.

With the quilt for a cape and the full moon for a spotlight, Sara stood at the window in her bedroom and intoned for an imaginary audience, "O Romeo, Romeo! Wherefore art thou, Romeo? Defy thy father and refuse thy name." And since that was all she could remember, she improvised from there.

Many a heroine was enacted that night under the full spotlight of the moon, until sleep dropped its gentle curtain, bringing an end to Sara's play.

Chapter Seven

Sara counted her change one more time. She had her heart set on the chocolates imported from England, but all she could afford were the chocolates from Montreal. Mrs. Lawson's eyes twinkled fondly as she waited patiently behind the counter for Sara to make up her mind.

Lawson's general store was busy that day, it being Tuesday, and Tuesday being the day the Avonlea Ladies Sewing Society met. The good ladies, whose duty it was to sew articles of clothing for the missions in China, sat comfortably around the stove.

"I'll take these, Mrs. Lawson," Sara finally said, resigned to the less glamorous treats. "Will you wrap them, please?"

"By all means, Sara. I even think I've got an extra length of silk ribbon somewhere we can use as a bow. Now, I won't be but a minute."

Mrs. Lawson bustled off to the back of the shop. Sara leaned against the counter, closed her eyes and breathed in the warm, spicy aroma of the general store. In her mind, she once again conjured up the fantasy of a theatrical life that she had been nurturing since Pigeon's arrival.

"If I were you, Theodora, I wouldn't stand for it another minute." Mrs. Spencer's sharp voice cut through Sara's dreams.

"But I love him," Theodora squeaked in her own defense. Her mousey-brown fly-away hair seemed to be bursting from its pins, as if it were expressing all the emotions she suppressed in her heart.

"What is love without a ring on your finger?" Mabel Sloane asked, threading her needle. "Either he proposes, or you get rid of him." As if to illustrate her point, she snapped the thread from its spool with her teeth.

"Get rid of him?" A look of deep horror

passed across Theodora's plain, good face.

"Yes. Find someone else." Mabel Sloane jabbed her needle through the cloth and pulled it forcefully through the other side.

"Maybe he needs more time," Theodora timidly suggested.

Mrs. Spencer threw her hands into the air and rolled her prominent eyes towards heaven. "Time! God created the world in seven days. Pat Frewen has had twenty years, and he's still just thinking about you."

Theodora cowered against her chair. She never was any good in an argument. Hers was a gentle character that had trouble standing up against those more forceful.

"But, I love him," was all she could manage.

Theodora knew her own heart. Although outwardly meek and fearful of conflict, once she made up her mind about something, she clung to it stubbornly, like moss on a rock.

"Theodora Dixon —" Mabel Sloane began. But the conversation was too much for the meek Theodora. She wished everyone would quit telling her what to do. The advice was overwhelming.

Feeling that she would suffocate if she stayed

any longer, Theodora jumped up, interrupting Mabel as she began her well-intentioned counsel, and bolted out the door, neglecting her coat and even her hat. The embroidery she had so meticulously and lovingly been working on flew from her lap, sailed through the air and fluttered down by Sara's feet. Sara picked it up and called after her, but the hapless Theodora was out the door before she could hear.

The icy touch of winter could be felt in that gray November day. Sara buttoned her coat against the raw autumn wind. She looked around, but Miss Dixon was nowhere to be found.

The brown ghosts of fallen leaves swirled and danced in the air. They swished and crunched under Sara's feet as she set out in search of Theodora Dixon. Turning off the main street, she saw her in front of the blacksmith's shop, pacing in circles and gesturing loudly, silently pleading her case to an imaginary jury.

"Miss Dixon, you dropped your embroidery."

Theodora jumped a bit, startled by the unexpected voice. Then she turned to face the speaker.

It was a mournful visage Sara saw. Theodora's

normally timid eyes now burned bright with anxiety. Her cheeks were pale and her thin, sharp nose was red and pinched by the cold.

"Oh Sara," Theodora groaned, taking the needlework in her chapped, red hand, "what good is embroidery? I might as well burn my hope chest." Theodora heaved a heavy sigh and then spoke the words she had been avoiding for twenty years. "Pat Frewen will never marry me."

"You can't give up."

"Well, that's just it," Theodora confided in her matter-of-fact way. "I never have given up. Ever since I first met that man twenty years ago, I knew he was the only one for me. I've been very patient. The only thing I worry about is that everybody else is right and he really is a lost cause."

"No, Theodora, he's only a lost cause when you stop trying." Sara had read that sentiment in a story and was pleased to have found a suitable occasion for it.

"Trying? I've tried everything under the sun. What do you think, Sara? What would you do?"

Sara had never really considered what she would do in a situation such as this. Actually, it had never occurred to her that the man she loved would not be just as happy to love her in return.

Plans started to form in her mind, but a small voice inside told her that she shouldn't meddle. In tone and inflection, the voice sounded surprisingly like Aunt Hetty's.

"Well ..." Sara hesitated, knowing her little voice was right, "... it's really none of my business."

Theodora's face fell. The little spark of hope she had been fanning died.

Sara felt terrible and ashamed to have been the cause of such great disappointment. Her desire to be helpful quickly hushed the nagging inner voice that kept telling her not to interfere.

"I've got to get going. I'm a guest for tea," Sara said proudly. "But I'll think about it," she offered, seeing no possible harm in that.

"You will?" The spark of hope rekindled in Theodora's face, brightening its dull melancholy.

Sara, glad to be the cause of such pleasure, went one step further. "I promise I'll try to think of something."

Theodora grabbed both of Sara's hands and squeezed them hard. "Oh, bless you, Sara. You are not like the others. Oh, but I mustn't keep you."

"Bye, Miss Dixon." Sara hurried back to the store to retrieve the chocolates. The chill autumn air did not touch her, for she was filled with the warmth of knowing that she was doing a good deed.

Chapter Eight

If ever a man favored his animals, Pat Frewen did, for he bore a marked resemblance to his pigs. He was a portly, balding man, with a small, snubbed nose and beady, deep-set eyes. His receding chin often bristled with a three-days' growth, and his clothing and hair were always messy and unkempt.

Pigs are too often maligned, and are considered by people who don't know them to be filthy and slovenly. But, underneath their rough exteriors, if anybody cared to look, they would find that pigs possess a keen intelligence and a loyal disposition. So, too, with Pat Frewen.

Twenty years ago, Pat Frewen fell in love with Pigeon Plumtree. It was in Charlottetown. From the moment he looked upon her, he knew she was the woman for him. Of course, she was totally unaware of his love. He fell in love with her from the audience; she was on the stage. He was so smitten that he went back every night to see her in the same play. By the end of its two-week run, he knew every line of dialogue.

Each night, after the performance, he would wait for her outside the stage door. He wanted to declare his love for her, propose marriage. But so did many other young men who waited with flowers and candy for her to appear after the performance. When Pigeon did appear, they jostled and shoved and called for her attention. Poor Pat was often pushed to the back of the crowd.

On the night of the last performance, Pat managed to elbow his way to the front of the crowd and hand Pigeon the bouquet of wild-flowers he had picked before the show. Pigeon smiled at him, briefly. Pat wanted to speak to her, but he was too shy. For twenty years he kicked himself for not having said what was on his mind. Over the years Pat forgot the exact words he had wanted to say, but he never forgot her smile.

When the play's run was over and Pigeon left

Charlottetown, Pat remained faithful to her in his heart. All these years he had kept the playbill from the performance, folded and protected in his dresser drawer. He knew one day he'd meet her again, and when he did, he would tell her his feelings.

About that same time, he met Theodora Dixon at a box social. She took a shining to him, which he neither encouraged nor discouraged. He never formally courted her, but he never rejected the friendship she offered, either. Over the years, he got used to her company and enjoyed the evenings they spent together. Theodora was a good woman, and Pat appreciated all the little things she did for him, the care she took. But, years ago, he had made up his mind that Pigeon Plumtree was the woman for him, and to this notion Pat remained loyal.

As the years passed by, Pat grew accustomed to courting his sweetheart in his imagination. The dreams of her and the life they would live together had become so real that her miraculous arrival in Avonlea—her actual physical presence, like a princess conjured from his dreams—came as a great shock to Pat.

He spent a sleepless night after her arrival,

torn between deep despair and great hope. One little voice in his head was convinced that all he needed to do was speak his piece to her and she would be his wife, just as he had rehearsed many a time in his dreams. But a second little voice kept calling him a fool, reminding him that she didn't know him from Adam.

By the time dawn arrived with her chilly grayness, Pat had made up his mind. As soon as he fed his pigs, he was going over to the White Sands Hotel to have a word with Miss Plumtree.

Chapter Nine

With the chocolates held snugly under her arm, Sara skipped towards the White Sands Hotel and her rendezvous with Pigeon. Her mind was so full of how wonderful the afternoon was going to be that she didn't see Pat Frewen until she'd almost careened into him.

"Mr. Frewen," she gasped, stopping just in time to prevent a collision, "what are you doing out here?"

Pat Frewen glanced around with the confused look of a man abruptly awakened from sleep. "Oh ... I'm just out for a ..." he paused for a moment and rooted around until he came up with the word he wanted, "... for a stroll, that's it."

The truth of the matter was that Pat had been skulking around the White Sands since morning, trying to get his courage up to talk to Pigeon Plumtree. Although he had started out with the firmest of intentions, as he got closer to the hotel, his courage faltered. He was very close to going home, giving up his long-held dreams.

"I'm going to pay a visit to my cousin, Miss Plumtree, the famous actress," Sara proudly told him. "She's staying at the White Sands Hotel."

Pat's face turned crimson, his jaw dropped, his eyes glazed over. In short, he was stupefied. "Pigeon Plumtree's your cousin? Don't that beat all!" He took off his cap. Scratching his head, Pat humphed and mumbled to himself in private debate, heedless of Sara's presence.

Sara watched him for a minute, not knowing whether it was more rude to stand there gawking or to go. She remembered her promise to Theodora and decided that this was as good a time as any to broach the subject.

Sara began with the utmost delicacy, for she

realized that in matters such as these, great care was called for.

"Mr. Frewen, I've been thinking about you. I know all about your problem."

"You do?" Pat asked, afraid he might have been pondering louder than he'd intended.

"I think you've been thinking about a certain lovely lady," Sara ventured.

Pat colored, embarrassed that she had guessed his secret. "Go on," he said gruffly.

"I think you've been thinking for so long that you must be confused."

Was this child a mind reader? Pat wondered. But the need to share his burden was so powerful that it made him confess. "I got her on the brain somethin' awful. It's makin' me real nervous."

"I take it you've never spoken to her directly about your feelings."

"Not what you would say is directly."

"Well, how is she going to know how you feel?" Sara asked, a little impatiently.

Pat knew she was right. He just didn't have the courage. "There's no use in that," he argued.

"You know what I think, Mr. Frewen? I think you should follow your heart and court the lady."

"Court her? I couldn't do that." By now he

❧❧❧

For twenty years, Theodora had been bent on becoming Pat Frewen's wife. Folks gathered at the pigpen each year as much to see whether Theodora had snagged him yet as to see his pigs take the blue ribbon.

❦

"Pat Frewen's the name. It was me that wrote
that, uh...that letter."
"You? You are not at all what I...what I expected."
Pigeon remained calm in spite of the shock.

❧❧❧

Pigeon bowed graciously to the audience.
"Thank you, thank you, one and all.
On behalf of my cousin Sara Stanley and myself,
I wish to make a personal donation."

❧❧❧❧❧

The audience burst into thunderous applause.
To everyone's great relief, the longest running drama
in Avonlea ended happily after all.

was convinced that he wasn't good enough for a woman as fine as Pigeon Plumtree. "She wouldn't have me."

"Oh, Mr. Frewen," Sara gushed sincerely, "you are wrong. She's in love with you. Deeply in love with you," she added, with just the proper degree of emotion. "She has been for twenty years. She even remembers the first time she laid eyes on you. She confided in me. It was love at first sight," Sara concluded, knowing that Theodora wouldn't mind if she betrayed her confidence.

So, that smile at the stage door had meant something, and his little bouquet had touched her after all! He wanted to shout with joy, but Pat Frewen was a cautious man and knew how to play his cards close to his chest.

"I don't mind tellin' you that I also find her mighty attractive," Pat confessed with a certain nonchalance.

"Well, that's all fine and good, but she just assumes that you're not interested," Sara chided.

"That's wrong," he yelped, and then he confided, "I—I—I just don't know what to do. I mean, where do I start?"

"Aunt Hetty has a book of etiquette at home,

and there's a chapter on courting. I'll bring it over as soon as possible."

"Do you think it will work?"

"Don't worry about a thing, Mr. Frewen. I'll fix everything. Well, I mustn't keep Miss Plumtree waiting," Sara added with a wink. "I'll see you later, Mr. Frewen."

Sara departed for her appointment, pleased that she could be of such help.

How long he stood there he couldn't say. Inside, he felt a tumult of hope and rapture mixed with a dash of fear.

The sun was low in the sky when Pat Frewen danced a jig with the trees, the clouds and a lone cow, the only witnesses to his joy.

Chapter Ten

"But she doesn't look the least bit like me," Sara protested, examining again the dark-haired, rather fat woman in the photograph.

"Outwardly, oh no. No, inwardly," Pigeon explained, taking the portrait of Great Aunt Eugenie in its ornate silver frame and placing it back on the table, as if further elaboration were unnecessary.

Sara was still quite baffled. In fact, much of what her cousin said that day confused her. "Inwardly?"

Pigeon's face became serious and her voice dropped to a deep whisper. She swooped close to Sara, grabbed her hands and looked deep into her eyes. "The spirit, the fire, the charm," she intoned, her words thick with intensity, "you have it all. I see it in your eyes."

Sara thrilled with excitement. She knew she had talent—all she needed was for it to be recognized.

Pigeon nestled back among the plump satin pillows on her chair. Sara was dying to hear more about her own natural acting abilities, but Pigeon said nothing further. She only smiled and studied Sara through half-closed eyes.

Sara grew uncomfortable under Pigeon's scrutiny and let her own eyes roam around the room. It was a jumble of expensive clothes, hats, knick-knacks and photographs, thrown recklessly here and there.

"Did you know that Eugenie was the world's most renowned expert on dying?" Pigeon asked.

"Dying?" Sara, startled, turned her gaze once again to her cousin.

Pigeon suddenly lunged from her chair. Her eyes took on a distracted look while her countenance contorted in a rictus of grief. "Yea, noise?" she croaked, her hand briefly cupping her ear then frantically clutching her heart. "Then, I'll be brief. O happy dagger!" Pigeon grabbed the butter knife from the table and held it aloft. "This is thy sheath; there rest, and let me die."

Before Sara could stop her, Pigeon had thrust the butter knife into her heart, wavered, buckled, gasped, then collapsed onto the chaise longue in a dead faint.

"Pigeon!" Sara screamed, leaping to her feet and running to her cousin's side. She expected the worst. "Are you all right?"

For one, eternal moment, there was no answer. Then Pigeon opened her eyes and laughed. "I'm fine, dear child. That was an Aunt Eugenie death scene," she explained, raising herself from the chaise and adjusting her hair. "Now you try it."

Pigeon had to rummage under several piles of clothing and through many suitcases before she could locate the text of *Romeo and Juliet*. She handed it to Sara.

Sara tried the scene as best as she could, but

her voice, she felt, sounded awkward and wooden. She was trying so hard to please that her own natural abilities were all choked up. When it came time to die, she stiffened and fell like a plank, flat out on the chaise longue. On the way down, she banged her head on a small table, which caused her to whisper a small "ouch," a bit of dialogue not found in the text.

The whole performance, in her opinion, was less than elegant. She would never be an actress, Sara felt with great despair.

"*Bravo!*" Pigeon clapped. "Now *that* was a death scene! Aunt Eugenie would be terribly proud."

"Pigeon, I'll never be as talented as you are," Sara wailed.

"Nonsense. You have inherited her magic, her cloak of greatness."

"Me?" Sara was reluctant to believe, but, somehow, Pigeon made everything seem possible.

Pigeon placed both hands on Sara's shoulders. "Poor child, your Aunt Hetty has provided you with such a dry little life here in Avonlea. It is my duty to enrich it. I see it clearly."

"My life isn't dry." Sara was taken aback. "Aunt Hetty does her best."

"Oh, of course she does," Pigeon cooed. "I only meant that the artistic soil is rather barren here. Surely your tender soul thirsts for some drama."

"I absolutely adore drama," Sara gushed.

"Then it's settled. I won't rest until I impart the world's oldest art form, the art of drama, to you."

"Pigeon, I'll work so hard. I'll make you proud of me, I will! I'm so excited, I could just cry!" And to prove it, Sara jumped up and down.

Pigeon grabbed her ecstatic protégée as if to steady her enthusiasm. "Darling child," she admonished, "never cry unless it's a part in a play. Crying ruins the eyes, and it makes one's nose a ghastly shade of red. Remember my motto: 'Shed no tears unless you are paid to do it.' I've cried far too much in my life."

"You've cried?" Sara was incredulous. "But, you have everything. What have you got to cry about?"

Pigeon turned her head away. Her features, momentarily clouded by a shadow of grief, quickly composed themselves. "Plenty!" She smiled sadly. "Parts I didn't get, children I didn't have, men I didn't marry ..."

"Were you ever in love?" Sara's voice was barely above a whisper.

Pigeon crossed to the window with tragic strides. Sara immediately regretted her question, fearing that she had been rude. Pigeon pulled back the curtain and looked longingly out the window, her lovely face lit by the late-afternoon sun.

Suddenly, she turned with a dramatic swirl and faced her young audience. "Was I ever in love?" she repeated quietly. "Only once that mattered. I was very young. He was very dashing," she added with a wry, wistful smile. "I turned him down because I wanted the stage more than I wanted him. I've lived to regret it."

Pigeon pulled a fine cambric handkerchief from her sleeve and dabbed the corner of each eye. Sara was much moved.

So excited was Sara that she started to run home that early autumn evening. But she soon caught herself and remembered one of the many bits of advice she had received that day. In Pigeon's accents, she repeated it out loud: "Remember, darling, the whole world's a stage with everyone watching. And on the stage, my dear, how one carries oneself is everything."

Chapter Eleven

Aunt Hetty, it seemed, had long ago lent the book of etiquette to Felicity. Sara knew she wasn't going to get the book back from her cousin without some reasonable explanation, so Sara, out of necessity, confided the whole scheme to her. Felicity, being of a romantic nature herself, was only too thrilled to be involved as an adviser in the courting of Theodora Dixon. She knew the etiquette book from cover to cover and was happy to share her many suggestions and much useful advice.

The brown grass was crackly with hoarfrost and the air smelled sharply of snow as the two self-appointed Cupids went on their errand in the service of true love.

Pat Frewen's barn was warm and dark, smelling of sweet hay and the acrid odor of pigs. He dumped another bucket of slop in the trough and watched as his pigs greedily gobbled it down. His elation of the previous day was now riddled with doubts. In a word, he was suffering a good case of cold feet.

Pat had grown so comfortable with his fantasy of Pigeon that the thought of actually meeting her gave him the jitters. Besides, Theodora had come by the night before with some chicken pot pie she'd just happened to whip up, and the two had whiled away a cozy evening together. What more could a man want?

"Mr. Frewen!" Sara's voice shook him from his thoughts. "We brought that book on etiquette that I told you about."

Sara and Felicity stood in the doorway, their cheeks rosy from the cold and their eyes bright with anticipation.

"That's awful nice of you, Sara. But maybe we should forget the whole thing."

"But why, Mr. Frewen?" Sara cried, disappointment visible on her face.

"She'd never have me." The one doubt that had persisted all these years came out unchecked from Pat's mouth, much to his own surprise.

"Mr. Frewen," Felicity said, in a voice sounding remarkably like Aunt Hetty's. She had decided to take the matter into her own hands. "You must stand firm. This book has everything you could ever possibly want to know about courting. For example," she said, licking her finger and leafing through the pages, "there's a chapter in here on compliments. It says you are supposed to whisper sweet nothings into your lady friend's ear."

"What's a sweet nothing?" Pat asked.

Felicity had been hoping he wouldn't ask. She hesitated, not sure herself how to define the term. Grabbing the book, Sara came to the rescue.

"There's one right here. It says, 'Dearest, your eyes are like violets.'"

Pat Frewen was a practical man. "Well, what if her eyes ain't like violets?"

Felicity looked to Sara for support, but even Sara was unnerved by the question.

"Well ..." she hesitated, "... I think you are supposed to say it anyway." She hoped she sounded like she knew what she was talking about.

Pat didn't look convinced. Felicity snatched the book from Sara and frantically turned the pages.

"Here's another chapter," she said, as cheerfully as possible, hoping to build up the man's confidence, "on 'The Art of Writing Love Letters.'"

"I couldn't do that," Pat protested.

"Oh, but you must," Sara insisted. "It's a terribly romantic thing to do."

"Listen to this." In her most romantic voice, Felicity read, "'Dearest one; As I sit here in the moonlight, thinking of your delicate face, your tender eyes, your flawless complexion ...'"

Felicity looked up from the page. Sentiments such as those were a bit too flowery, even for someone as sentimental as she was. But she remained optimistic. "There are lots of other ones in this chapter." She smiled and closed the volume. "We'll leave the book with you, and you can choose one that you like. How's that?"

Pat shook his head. The whole business was becoming overwhelming. "Thanks kindly, but I don't think I'm up to writing a letter."

"All you have to do is copy one out and send it to her. You'll sweep her off her feet, we promise," Felicity urged him.

Hope was once more kindled in the heart of Pat Frewen, bringing warmth to his cold feet. Maybe the girls were right. "Do you think it will work?"

"Of course it will," Sara said, a bit impatiently. She knew poor Theodora was just aching to hear any word from him. He was truly a pigheaded man, she concluded, taking the volume once more from her cousin and holding it out towards Pat.

He hesitated, coughed, rubbed his hands on his pants, shuffled a little, then finally accepted the book. As did the great Julius Caesar before him, Pat Frewen had now crossed his own Rubicon. There was no going back. Both girls heaved an audible sigh of relief.

"Oh, and, uh, Mr. Frewen," Sara said as candidly as possible, for the subject she was now approaching was a delicate one, "if I were you, I'd also read the chapter on how a gentleman should dress."

"What's wrong with the way I dress?" Pat demanded.

"Nothing much," Sara reassured him, not wanting to hurt his feelings. Then she added, with as much tact as she could muster, "I just think that your wardrobe could do with a little perking up, that's all."

"And if you don't mind my saying so," Felicity continued in the same manner, "I think you could invest in a shave, and perhaps even a hair-cut, too."

Pat Frewen shook his head and snorted. "I can see this courting business is going to set me back a bundle."

"Oh, but Mr. Frewen," Sara asserted, edging towards the barn door, "it's most important. Remember, 'Faint heart ne'er won fair lady,'" she quoted. The two girls slipped out the door and were away before Pat Frewen could offer more objections.

Pat stood for a moment considering all the advice he'd been given. "Well, Lulubelle," he said, slapping the back of his prize sow, "I guess if she's Pigeon Plumtree's cousin, she must know more than I do." And with that, he accepted the course laid out for him.

Chapter Twelve

Having acted as Cupid's messenger, Sara flew home as quickly as possible. The greatest part of her mission had been accomplished. The rest was just a matter of time.

A few random snowflakes had begun to fall by the time Sara entered Rose Cottage. The warmth of a fire in the parlor hearth felt cozy against her cold skin as she removed her hat and coat.

The cheerful fire was for the benefit of the biannual meeting of the Avonlea Improvement Society, an organization of civic-minded women dedicated to the beautification of Avonlea. Hetty King was hosting. Sara entered the parlor quietly just as Mrs. Spencer, the reigning president, was finishing her enumeration of the committee's many accomplishments.

Mrs. Spenser's voice rang out in authoritative tones. "And so, ladies, I am proud to say we have accomplished a great deal in the last year towards the beautification of our village and its surroundings."

Sara saw Theodora Dixon, who sat absorbed in the words of the speaker. Sara made her way towards the hapless woman, managing in the process to step on Mabel Sloane's foot and trip over Deirdre Sutherland's knitting basket.

"We've painted the school and replaced the plants around the town hall," Mrs. Spencer's voice boomed.

Poor Theodora nearly jumped out of her skin when Sara lightly touched her arm.

"Don't worry about your problem, Miss Dixon. Things are moving in the right direction," Sara whispered, more loudly than she had intended.

"Ahem." Mrs. Spencer cleared her throat in a very pointed manner. Sara looked up to see everyone staring at her and Miss Dixon. Theodora turned such a deep shade of crimson she was almost purple.

"Sara, please sit down and don't interrupt," Hetty ordered sharply, grabbing her niece by the arm and depositing her in a nearby chair.

Mrs. Spencer continued. "But we still have an eyesore to deal with. Perhaps, as treasurer, Theodora, you could elaborate."

Theodora rose nervously, almost knocking her chair over in the process. Mabel Sloane caught it before it fell.

"As you know," she began, her voice tense and high, for speaking to groups made her nervous, "ever since Thomas Bickle's barn burned to the ground he has not lifted a baby finger to clear the charcoal remains, let alone rebuild."

Great murmurs of indignation filled the room. Theodora took courage from the response and continued in a more forceful vein. "I'm afraid that we'll have to take matters into our own hands."

"Here, here"

"Unfortunately," Theodora cautioned, "even though we've already had a bake sale and a rummage sale, we are still short of funds. Does anyone have any fresh ideas as to how we could raise some more money?"

The room fell silent. Nobody moved; nobody raised a hand. Poor Theodora was afraid that her whole project would end up in disaster.

Sara raised her hand tentatively.

"Yes, Sara?" Theodora prompted, relief flooding her every feature.

"Maybe Miss Plumtree could give a recitation."

"Definitely not," Hetty snapped before anyone else could say anything.

"Everyone would pay to hear her, I'm sure of it," Sara protested.

"I wouldn't be too sure of that, Sara." Hetty smirked and looked around the room for agreement. There was none.

"What a wonderful idea, Sara!" Mrs. Spencer exclaimed. "It's a natural opportunity for an organization like ours to take advantage of.

Ladies, let's put it to a vote. Everyone in favor of asking Pigeon Plumtree to recite, raise your hands."

With only one exception, all hands shot up eagerly in agreement. Hetty King sat sourly with her hands tightly clasped in her lap. The eyes of every woman in the Improvement Society were upon her.

"Hetty?" Mrs. Spencer asked archly.

The pressure was too much to bear. With a disdainful gesture, Hetty unclasped one hand and raised it unwillingly in the air.

"Passed," Mrs. Spencer hollered as she brought down the gavel.

Sara was so excited that she could hardly wait until school ended the following day so that she could see Pigeon again. It had been two days since their tea together, and not a word had she heard from Pigeon about the acting lessons she had offered.

Sara had wanted to pay a visit earlier, but she'd been afraid to drop by uninvited. She certainly didn't want to wear out her welcome with her glamorous and generous cousin. The request of the Improvement Society gave Sara the perfect excuse to drop by, not for herself, but for a good cause.

To Sara's great delight, Pigeon was thrilled to see her. Although it was late afternoon, Pigeon was dressed in her satin dressing gown, reading a novel and eating chocolates.

Sara explained the purpose of her visit and spoke with great solemnity of the worthiness of the cause. Pigeon listened with a gentle amusement on her face and then assured her young cousin that she would be honored to recite for their "little barn burning."

"Barn raising," Sara corrected.

"Whatever. But darling, you tell your little Avonlea ladies that I will recite, provided, of course, that my dear, sweet Sara recites along with me."

"Oh, Pigeon!" Sara gasped. This was like a dream come true. "What shall I say? I'd be honored to."

"Good." Pigeon shut her novel and put it aside. Pushing up the sleeves of her dressing gown, she continued, "All the more reason to begin your acting lessons at once. You must come here every day after school."

So, for the rest of that glorious afternoon,

Sara listened while Pigeon recited her favorite scenes from plays and told more stories about the theater and theatrical life. It wasn't exactly an acting lesson, because Sara was only the audience. But Sara told herself that night, as she snuggled under the covers, that tomorrow, surely, she would begin her training.

Chapter Thirteen

Sara traipsed down the stairs one by one with a royal air, one hand on the bannister, the other extended gracefully. Her head was held high, her chin slightly tilted in the air. She entered the kitchen with a flourish, kissed her Aunt Olivia, who was having her morning coffee, then grandly took her place at the table.

"Morning, Sara," Hetty greeted her without turning from the stove. "Would you like some tea?"

"I'd love to, Hetty darling," Sara intoned, her voice deep and rich, "but tea is not good for the kidneys, don't you know."

Hetty spun quickly around. "Sara Stanley, I'll have you know that polite young ladies do not discuss their kidneys in public."

Either Sara did not hear, or she chose to ignore Hetty's rebuke. "Good morning, Olivia, dearest. And how are you this gorgeous morning?"

Olivia's velvet brown eyes twinkled with merriment and her full, red lips twitched into a smile. "I'm quite well," she replied, restraining her mirth. "And how's yourself?"

"Oh, marvelous, darling," Sara droned, drawing out each syllable.

"Gracious, child, whatever's got into you?" Hetty demanded, her hands on her hips.

"I, along with the famous Pigeon Plumtree, am going to recite for the Avonlea Improvement Society's fund-raiser."

"No, absolutely not!" Hetty protested. "I should have put my foot down the minute that woman breezed into my house and ate up all my good chocolates. Gin fizz, indeed."

It didn't take long for Hetty to work herself into a frenzy. She paced around the kitchen, gesturing wildly with both hands.

"Well, the Stanley side of the family are all a bunch of misfits, come to think of it. Especially the arty ones."

Sara watched her aunt quietly. "She won't recite unless I do. You don't want me to tell the

Improvement Society that you're against the fund-raiser, do you?"

Hetty stopped in her tracks. "No, no, I—I," Hetty spluttered. "Oh, have it your way. Charity is charity, I suppose. But I'm warning you, Sara, if you pursue this acting nonsense, that Pigeon person will have you running off, gallivanting halfway around the world like a—a gypsy!" Hetty crumpled the hem of her apron and brought it up to her mouth. Her eyes filled with tears.

"I wouldn't do that, Aunt Hetty." Sara's heart was filled with her aunt's sadness.

"No?" Hetty asked, her voice thick with sorrow. "That's what your mother said ... and off she went, every way the wind blew."

Hetty King had never forgiven Blair Stanley for taking Sara's mother away from Avonlea. To this day, Hetty believed that all of that traveling had led to her beloved younger sister's untimely death. And Hetty was not one to give up a grudge.

"Now, Hetty ..." Olivia said calmly, trying to soothe her.

"And before I know it, poof, you'll be gone too, just like your mother—and forever, no doubt."

There was the catch of a sob in Hetty's voice.

Sara watched, miserable, helpless against her aunt's grief. Hetty looked out the window, lost in her anguish. But as quickly as her sadness had appeared, it departed.

"Good grief," she exclaimed, without a trace of tears, "what is Pat Frewen doing lurking about out there?"

Sara jumped up from the table. "He's come to see me."

"What on earth for?"

Sara hurried into her coat, again putting on her airs. "The dear heart, he leads such a small, barren life. I feel it's my duty to enrich his dry little existence."

"That'll be quite enough of that patronizing affectation, Sara," Hetty scolded, but Sara only smiled. "And don't go bringing that man in here. I'll not have my house smelling like a barnyard."

Sara was already halfway out the door. "You needn't worry, darling. I'm on my way, then." Blowing a kiss, Sara dashed out the door before Hetty could chide her further.

Pat Frewen stood, lone and lorn, clutching the book of etiquette in one hand and a letter, neatly sealed, in the other. Once again, he was having misgivings.

"I wrote the little miss my love letter," he blurted out to Sara without even greeting her. "But, I'm feeling ... uh ... well, a bit awkward, you know, about ... actually mailing it."

Honestly, Sara thought to herself, a more reluctant fellow she had never met! Sara grasped the man firmly by the arm. "Mr. Frewen, you can't hold on to that letter forever. Just mail it."

Then she led him through the town until they could hand the *billet-doux* to Mr. Wilkins, the mailman.

"Now, Mr. Frewen," Sara suggested, "let's go for that haircut and shave we talked about. You can't go courting without a haircut. Come on."

Chapter Fourteen

Avonlea was bustling with its usual Saturday morning activity. A few people noticed Sara Stanley leading Pat Frewen along the main street, but most thought nothing of it until the pair turned the corner and headed for the shop with the red-and-white-striped pole. Then the news spread like wildfire over dry prairie grass as the townfolk scurried in excitement to inform their neighbors: "Can you believe it? Pat Frewen's at the barbershop, getting himself a shave."

Although many people might have noticed it, it was Mabel Sloane who first understood its significance. Or at least that's how she related it, taking the credit when she told and retold the tale.

Mabel had been in the general store, discussing the plans for the upcoming fund-raiser, when she'd seen them. Instantly, she had crushed her unsuspecting hat against her head and taken off, running as fast as her plump little legs would carry her.

Theodora Dixon pulled the freshly baked loaf from the oven. This was her favorite Saturday morning moment, sitting down to a slice of warm bread spread with homemade preserves, and a nice cup of tea.

The kitchen was toasty from the heat of the oven. Theodora's cheeks were flushed from the heat. She took her bread and her tea and settled herself in her favorite armchair by the fire. The flames crackled and roared. The ginger cat, who had been napping on the hearth, got up, stretched and yawned, then curled up once again on the braided rug and dropped quickly back to sleep. It was a pleasant moment, but how much more pleasant it would be if there were someone to share it with, she thought with a sigh.

Mabel Sloane pounded once on the door but was too excited to wait for a response. Opening the door herself, she charged into the parlor without so much as a howdy-do.

"Theodora, come quickly," Mabel gasped. Her eyes were wild and her hat, squashed forever out of shape, was jammed firmly on her head. "Pat Frewen went into the barbershop. He's getting a *shave!*"

"No." Theodora gasped, and her hands flew to her face.

"And a haircut," Mabel added.

The crowd was three rows deep in front of the window of the barbershop when Theodora arrived. "Let her through, let her through," Mabel ordered. When they saw who it was, the spectators parted and let Theodora take the best view.

She pressed her forehead against the cold glass and cupped her hands around her face to cut down the glare. Once her eyes had adjusted to the dimmer light within, Theodora could see that the rumor was true. There in the chair, a white cloth tucked under his chin, sat Pat Frewen, his face half obscured by lather.

Several people congratulated her. Theodora's heart fluttered with joy. It never occurred to her, or anybody else, that Pat Frewen would spruce himself up for anyone other than Theodora.

Once his cheeks were smooth and smelled sweetly of cologne, Pat decided he rather liked this self-improvement. Catching sight of a display of hairpieces of various shapes and colors, he inquired, "How much?"

"Well," the barber drawled, "seeing as how you're going courting, and seeing as I'm only through here every couple of weeks ..." The barber paused while he considered the deal. "Fifty cents, my best possible price," he announced.

Pat thought that a bit steep, but Sara nodded, urging him to accept.

"Whew, this courtin' rigmarole sure eats into

a pocketbook," Pat complained as he reached for his money.

When Pat rose from the chair, the crowd dispersed. By the time he walked out of the shop, activity on the street was back to normal, with people strolling casually to and fro, going about their accustomed business. More than one set of eyes, however, watched as Pat and Sara walked into Lawson's general store.

At Lawson's, Pat bought a bowler hat and a brand new cravat.

"You won't be sorry you spent your money on your appearance, Mr. Frewen," Sara urged him. "You look quite the gentleman."

Pat, admiring himself in the mirror, had to agree.

"Well, I'd better hurry," Sara said, satisfied with her day's work. "Miss Plumtree's giving me acting lessons. I don't want to be late."

Pat bent down and, in a conspiratorial whisper, entreated her, "You say hello to her for me." Then he winked.

"I will." Sara winked back, though she wasn't quite sure why.

Chapter Fifteen

"More milk, Sara," Pigeon demanded.

Sara lifted the porcelain pitcher from the marble-topped table and poured its warm contents into the iron bathtub. Pigeon splashed and cooed as she wallowed in the milky waters of her bath.

"Thank you. Dab some on your face, dear," Pigeon suggested as she daintily dotted her own face with the softening liquid. "Remember, in the theater, your face is your fortune."

"Aunt Hetty says that beauty is only skin deep," Sara replied uncertainly.

"Yes, well, Cleopatra bathed in milk, and she went a tad further in life than your Aunt Hetty. Bathe in milk once a day, darling, and you will have skin like a baby's bottom," Pigeon sang out in that cheerful tone she used when imparting wisdom, which she did quite frequently.

Sara turned her attention back to the volume of poetry she held in her lap. She was beginning to tire of Pigeon's wisdom. For the last few days, instead of instruction in the art of drama, all Sara seemed to receive was advice—on everything from what to wear to how to tell the difference between a baron and a duke. Sara was beginning to wonder whether Pigeon would keep her promise about giving her acting lessons.

She also was beginning to worry. The recital for the Improvement Society was only a week away, and they still hadn't picked out anything to read.

"Here's one, Pigeon." Sara cleared her throat and began to read. "'A thing of beauty is a joy forever. Its loveliness increases; it will never pass into nothingness.'"

"Exquisite, darling. I do adore Keats. Do you think I should wear the mauve taffeta or the peach moiré?"

Sara decided to be blunt. "I need you to help me choose a reading for the recital."

"Well, pick something out, memorize it and repeat it for me next lesson. Meanwhile, it's time for you to learn elocution."

"Elocution?"

"The art of speaking, dearest. Absolutely essential for an actor. Now, repeat after me: Betty Botter bought some butter. 'But,' said she, 'this butter's bitter.'"

"Betty Botter bought some butter."

"Enunciate, darling, enunciate."

"'But', said she, 'this butter's bitter.'"

"The voice, darling, the voice."

And so, for all intents and purposes, Sara finally received her first acting lesson.

That evening, Sara practiced and practiced her elocution until she had all of the tongue-twisters down perfectly. She couldn't wait to show Pigeon how hard she had worked. It was her fondest wish to make Pigeon proud of her.

After dinner, Sara went through every volume of poetry she could get her hands on until she found a fitting piece. It was a difficult choice, but Sara finally decided that Browning's "Incident at French Camp" would be her selection, for it contained all of the elements Sara associated with drama: heroic characters, exciting action and a noble but tragic ending.

The next day, bright and early, Sara dressed in her best pinafore and brushed her hair one hundred strokes until it was soft and shiny.

At breakfast, she recited her tongue-twisters so many times that she drove her poor Aunt

Hetty to distraction, and even tried the patience of gentle Olivia.

Hetty had had her fill of that Plumtree woman five minutes after she had set foot in her house. Now she resented the influence she seemed to be having on Sara. She didn't like her niece putting on airs and prancing about like a duchess.

Deep down, in a place so hidden she wasn't even aware it existed, Hetty was jealous. And yes, a little scared. Jealous that Pigeon had Sara's affection, and afraid that she might lose her dear niece forever. But for Hetty King, fear was a sign of weakness, and jealousy a signpost on the road to perdition. Since she couldn't admit to those feelings, what Hetty King chose to show was annoyance.

"Sara Stanley, I've had enough of your gibberish," Hetty declared after the tenth rendition of "Betty Botter."

"Pigeon says that practice makes perfect."

"Practice makes perfect, indeed. You'd be better off doing your homework, my girl, which, I might add, has been sadly neglected since that ridiculous woman came to town."

"Pigeon says I can do homework any time.

Right now I have special abilities that need to be," and here Sara did her best imitation of Pigeon's tones, drawing out the vowels and letting the "r"s roll from her tongue, "*nur-r-r-tur-r-red.*"

"Oh, and she's the only one that can *nur-r-r-tur-r-re* them?" Hetty mimicked.

Sara didn't bother to reply. "May I be excused?" she asked quietly.

"Yes," Olivia answered, advising Hetty with a glance to let the matter drop.

Hetty crossed her arms over her chest, tapped her foot and shut her mouth so tight that her lips disappeared. She stayed that way until Sara left the house.

As soon as they were alone, Olivia scolded her older sister. "You've done nothing but criticize Pigeon Plumtree, morning, noon and night. And where has it got you? Nowhere."

Hetty, refusing to answer, just tapped her foot and fumed.

Sara arrived at the White Sands Hotel late in the morning. Pigeon was barely out of bed and was still wearing her dressing gown, lounging over her morning coffee. Sara, anxious to continue her acting lessons, waited with thinly veiled impatience as Pigeon made her way through a pile of toast with marmalade.

By the time Pigeon had finished her toast and was beginning her third cup of coffee, Sara's patience had reached its limit.

"We have to rehearse for the recital, Pigeon."

"In a minute, dearest," Pigeon replied, her attention miles away. Pigeon picked up her mail and began to rifle through it.

Sara squirmed and fidgeted. She tried once more for Pigeon's attention. "I chose 'Incident at French Camp.'" Sara cleared her throat and began to recite: "'You know we French stormed Ratisbonne —'"

"Lovely, darling," Pigeon interrupted, scrutinizing a letter. The handwriting was not familiar to her. Taking her knife she eagerly opened it. Like all incurable romantics, somewhere deep in her heart Pigeon believed in the letter that might one day change her life.

Sara was more than miffed. Tears of anger crept into her eyes, but she blinked them back.

"Well, well, well. Sara," Pigeon turned her full attention to her for the first time that morning, "it seems I have an admirer here in Avonlea. A charming and cultured one."

Pigeon read greedily through the letter, gobbling up every word.

"Oh, merciful God," Pigeon gasped, bringing her hand to her throat. "He wants to lunch with me today! Good heavens, I must get dressed, immediately!"

With a flurry and a flutter, Pigeon flew around the room, grabbing first this dress then that, discarding everything she touched as unacceptable.

"But you said practice makes perfect," Sara reminded her, the disappointment heavy in her words.

"I did? Well, darling, I can't let a little rehearsal for your silly little—what, what is it?— Improvement Society, keep me from meeting a gentleman of this calibre." Pigeon settled on the black gabardine suit and the cream-colored blouse with the French lace.

"But you said the show must go on!"

"Well, of course it must, darling. But, darling, surprise little lunches like these don't often happen to a lonely thespian like myself. You never know where they may lead. Now, darling, run along. The show will have to wait."

Sorely disillusioned, Sara left. Pigeon, caught

up in her own ambitions, didn't even notice her
exit.

Chapter Sixteen

In spite of her beauty, her success and her
talent, Pigeon Plumtree was a lonely woman.
She had come to Avonlea wishing to ease her
loneliness through Sara. She was hoping the
child's affection would act as a solace to the bar-
renness of her life. Although Sara was a dear
child, Pigeon's heart still ached with an empti-
ness that not even Sara could fill.

The mysterious letter, with its promise of
romance, filled the aching void in Pigeon's heart
with hope. She felt like a young schoolgirl,
giddy and bursting with nerves over this
impending rendezvous with what she could
only hope would be her bright destiny.

By the time she had finished dressing, Pigeon
not only had an image in her mind of the mysterious gentleman, she also had their whole
future together planned. He would be rich, of
course, and tall. That he was a gentleman and
cultured she had no doubt. She anticipated
being very happy with him. Pigeon put on her

yellow kid gloves and, with her heart full of hope, went down to the dining room of the White Sands Hotel.

Pat Frewen had finished his chores early that morning. He'd been so jittery he could barely hold the handle of the slop bucket. After he had fed the pigs, he'd sat down to his own breakfast, but he couldn't eat much. His stomach was too full of butterflies.

As the morning drew on to lunchtime, he shaved himself, patted on the cologne he'd bought and took Grandpa Frewen's funeral suit out of the mothballs. The suit was a bit worn in the elbows but, generally, it was in good shape. And it fit, too. Even though it was a tad old, Pat had seen no need to buy himself a new one.

Once his suit was on, and his new cravat neatly tied, Pat reached into a box for the finishing touch. Taking the hairpiece, he gingerly set it on his bald head. It took several adjustments to get it in just the right place, but once it was settled, Pat was mighty pleased. With his new head of hair, he felt like a new man. Pigeon Plumtree, he thought, would be proud to be courted by him.

For twenty years he had dreamt of this woman, and now he would finally make his dream come true. Pat Frewen made a final adjustment to his new hair, brushed off his suit one last time and, clutching the etiquette book under his arm, set off for the White Sands Hotel, his heart full of hope.

It had been two days since Pat Frewen had visited the barbershop, and still he hadn't come to call. But Theodora Dixon remained patient. After all, she had waited twenty years—what was two more days? she thought as she hurried on her way to the meeting of the planning committee of the Avonlea Improvement Society. She had taken special care with her attire, as she had the day before, and as she would continue to do, so that when Pat did propose, she would look her best.

Theodora flew up the path to Mabel Sloane's house. For the past two days, her feet had hardly touched the ground.

"My dear, you look radiant," Mrs. Sloane gushed once Theodora was inside.

Theodora smiled and her eyes sparkled with joy. It was true, her excitement had given a glow to her cheeks and smoothed the worry from her face.

"Has he...?" Mabel Sloane inquired.

"Not yet." Theodora blushed.

"It is only a matter of time" was the consensus of the planning committee, for it was a foregone conclusion that Pat was on the verge of popping the question.

As soon as they had concluded the business at hand—putting the finishing touches on the plans for the recital—the committee set off altogether for the White Sands Hotel to make sure the hotel manager had made the proper arrangements. In the midst of this bevy, led by Hetty King, went Theodora Dixon, her heart full of hope.

Along the way they ran into Sara, trudging home from her disappointing visit with Pigeon. She would make a fool of herself at this recital, she was sure. People would want their money back, and Thomas Bickle's barn would never be rebuilt.

She had herself so thoroughly convinced that her performance was going to be a disaster that she almost hid in shame when she saw the planning committee heading her way.

They were delighted to see her and asked several times how her recital piece was progressing.

"Quite well," Sara said, almost choking on the words. She thought it best to keep her fears to herself.

"You'd best come with us, child," said Hetty. "You'll know, I suppose, whether they've set up the hall properly for ... whatever it is you and the Plumtree woman are planning to do."

So, with nothing but despair in her heart, Sara set off with the others towards the White Sands Hotel.

Chapter Seventeen

"I'm waiting for someone, a gentleman," Pigeon informed the maître d'hotel as she settled herself at the table. "Send him this way, if you please."

"Very well, madam." The maître d' bowed and slipped away from the table.

Pigeon looked around the crowded dining room. There was no one there who fitted the image in her mind. She settled herself into her chair, picked up the menu and waited.

"Very good, Miss King." The hotel manager gave her a courteous nod. "Though I think you can expect a greater crowd than fifty. Many of our guests expressed an interest in hearing Miss Plumtree recite, you know."

Sara's heart fell. More than fifty people there to see her make a fool of herself. She wanted to run away right then and there.

A loud gasp from Theodora made her change her mind.

It seemed that the moment Theodora had been dreaming about for twenty years had finally arrived. Theodora felt all fluttery inside. Her happiness spread across her face in a wide smile. Her heart raced with excitement. Never before had she felt such joy. Around her, the planning committee all whispered their congratulations. For entering the hotel lobby, decked out in his Sunday best and carrying a bouquet of flowers, was Pat Frewen.

Sara forgot her own misery. At least one of her plans was going to be successful!

Theodora waited, her eyes bright with anticipation. Surrounded by the members of the planning committee, Theodora watched as the man she loved crossed the hotel lobby. Any second now he would approach her.

She was more than a little surprised when

Pat, instead of crossing the length of the lobby to address her, turned and entered the dining room instead. Her eyes were still shiny, but her brow wrinkled into puzzlement. Her smile, lately so wide, drooped to a narrow frown.

Sara tugged at her sleeve. "Let's follow him."

"Uh ... ahem, Miss Plumtree? How'd you do?"

Pigeon looked up from the menu. "Good day," she responded, wondering who this impertinent little man could be.

"Pleased to make your acquaintance." Pat bowed, just as the etiquette book had instructed. "Kiss your hand, madam?"

"My good man," she said graciously, for she could afford to be gracious, "I'm expecting a guest."

"Oh, that's me. Pat Frewen's the name. It was me that wrote that, uh ... that letter."

Theodora and Sara entered the dining room just in time to witness the scene. Theodora, utterly humiliated, her hopes now dashed, was furious. Sara was stunned. And she wasn't the only one.

"You? You are not at all like what I ... what I would have expected." Pigeon remained calm in spite of the shock. "What exactly do you do?"

"I'm a farmer, a pig farmer to be specific. Best pork in Prince Edward Island." Pat tried to keep the nervousness from his voice. "Now, I hear by the grapevine that you've been pining for me for twenty years. Well, I just want to take this opportunity to let you know that the feeling is mutual."

Pat nodded his head so vigorously that his hairpiece, which wasn't well anchored to begin with, came loose from its moorings. Gently it sailed down from his head and landed smack dab in the middle of the white china plate. It rested there, looking like some large, hairy insect.

Pat was mortified. He found himself wondering what the etiquette book would say to do in a situation such as this.

Pigeon picked the errant hairpiece from her plate. Daintily, she held it aloft for all to see. As cool as a cucumber, she offered it back to its owner.

"Stop right there. I believe you have dropped something. I suggest you take it and leave. Never," she said with the voice of a duchess, "would a highly acclaimed professional like myself be the slightest bit interested in someone of your ilk ... no matter how remarkable your pork."

Pat was flabbergasted. This was not the way he had dreamed it would go. "But, but, we have a lot in common!" was all he could think of to say.

"Ha! You must be dreaming," she replied, with mocking laughter.

It was true, Pat realized as the bitter laughter echoed in his ears. He had been dreaming all these years. She wasn't the woman for him. Theodora Dixon was a better woman than her, and a good companion, too. Why had he been so blind? Theodora was the woman he should marry.

Gathering his shattered pride, Pat turned with what dignity remained to him and started out of the dining room. His intention was to march right over to Theodora to propose. He might as well do it now, he figured, since he already had his suit on. It would be a shame to waste a good bouquet of flowers, too.

Pat didn't have to go very far to find Theodora. She was standing in the doorway to the dining room. From the look of fury on her face, he guessed that she had witnessed the whole thing. That was the final humiliation.

"You're nothing but a two-timer," Theodora spluttered, her face twisted with anger.

"Theodora, wait. I can explain!"

Theodora didn't want to wait. She had waited too long as it was. With her hands over her face to catch her tears, Theodora ran out of the White Sands Hotel.

Sara witnessed the drama, sick with misery. Her meddling, she realized, had caused the whole thing. From the dining room she could hear the ring of Pigeon's hysterical laughter.

Chapter Eighteen

Sara found Pat sitting on a stone bench in the churchyard. He made a sorrowful figure, perched on that cold, gray stone, silhouetted against a bleak November sky. His face was blank, his eyes stared dismally, his shoulders were hunched up as if to carry the weight of his miseries.

The hollow wind rattled the empty trees. Sara shivered. It wasn't going to be pleasant, but she knew what she must do.

"Mr. Frewen," Sara blurted, "I feel awful about this. It's all my fault."

Pat looked up and smiled gently at the girl who stood so bravely at his side. "Naw, it's as much my fault as it is yours. I went and wrote that letter."

"I never dreamed that you—that you meant to court Miss Plumtree. I thought that you were hoping to court Theodora Dixon."

"Oh Sara, I made a fool of myself. It's like I saw it all in an instant. Theodora's the woman I love. But I didn't know it until I lost her. Probably lost her forever. I've only got myself to blame."

Sara felt sick at heart. She knew that she shouldn't interfere any more to help poor Pat and Theodora. She'd done enough damage already. But there was one thing she knew she had to do.

"Come in," Pigeon called in response to the knock on her door.

Sara entered the hotel room. Pigeon was draped luxuriously over the chaise longue. Her shoes, carelessly discarded, lay scattered on the floor. Her hair was loosened, as were her corset stays. Several plump pillows nestled by her side.

"Come in, child," she called, with a gaiety that sounded more shrill than joyous.

Sara solemnly sat on the edge of a chair. She gazed at her cousin with serious, steady eyes.

"Sara, darling, why did you leave the hotel so suddenly today?"

Sara remained silent. Pigeon found it a bit unnerving. "Where is your sense of humor, child?" she teased.

"There was nothing funny in what you said to Mr. Frewen, Pigeon. Embarrassing him like that in front of all those people."

Pigeon laughed, a harsh, forced laugh. "But Sara, think of what a funny stage play it would make. This pathetic little pig farmer from nowhere presuming that he can court someone of my renown." Pigeon burst into renewed laughter. "It really is delicious, darling, don't you see? What a divine little farce." Pigeon's mouth remained in a ridiculous grin, but her eyes were dark with a hidden sorrow.

"But that's just it, Pigeon. It isn't a stage!" Sara admonished her. "You could have at least spoken to him kindly. He's a real person, and you hurt his feelings."

"Oh, dear heart —"

Sara could not hold back her own tears. "You're always saying 'dear heart' this and 'darling child' that, but you don't mean it. You don't really care about me. The only person you care about is yourself."

With great dignity, Sara rose. The tears trickled down her cheeks but her face remained composed. Solemnly, she walked to the door and, with stately decorum, made her exit.

The curtain had been lifted and illusions shattered. Sara now saw her cousin for what she truly was—a self-centered, shallow person.

Chapter Nineteen

Pigeon stared at herself in the mirror. All the masks were gone, laying bare the pain. The child had spoken the truth. And the truth, Pigeon thought, smiling wryly at her own reflection, hurts.

Her behavior had been abominable, that was true. There was no excuse for it. It was a shameful, horrible way to act, to humiliate that poor man so. Even the knowledge of her own pain, her own loneliness and her own disappointment did not excuse her performance in the hotel dining room. It had been, she decided, one of her worst roles.

She was not by nature a cruel person. A tad selfish, perhaps, and, over the course of the years, grown a bit callous—but not cruel. She despised cruelty.

Losing the esteem of that remarkable child was what hurt her the most. She had had such plans. She had wanted to lavish affection on the child, do so much for her, give her everything. Reviewing the past week, Pigeon realized that she had not given anything at all.

There were a few things that she could do now to patch up the damage she'd caused. First, however, she must try to make amends to Sara.

Hetty King hadn't the heart to scold her niece or to even say "I told you so." The poor child was taking it so hard—that was punishment enough.

Sara sat in the parlor, an open book unread on her lap. As if to match her mood, the gray skies had turned to rain, and Sara watched it as it trickled down the window pane.

"Sara," Hetty announced, "you have a visitor."

A subdued Pigeon entered the room. Sara
stared at her briefly, her face a mask, then turned
back to look out the window.

"Please," Pigeon implored, and for once she
sounded sincere, "just listen to what I have to
say." Pigeon settled on the divan. She patted the
cushion for Sara to join her. Reluctantly, Sara
went over and perched stiffly beside her.

Pigeon took both of Sara's hands in hers.
"You were right about the way I acted. It grieves
me, the way I behaved. I've spent so many years
play-acting that I forget what is real and what
isn't."

Sara nodded in agreement.

"In a play, you see, the emotion is not real.
The pain only lasts until the curtain falls. When I
play-act, I don't have to feel my own pain, my
own loneliness." Pigeon's voice faltered a bit. "I
can forget it exists." With a great effort, she
blinked back the tears and forced a smile.

Once more, Sara saw her cousin in a new
light. She was more moved by this performance
than any other she had seen, because it was real
and from the heart.

"Oh, please forgive me," Pigeon entreated,
her tone genuine, her emotion unfeigned. "Is

there any way I can prove to you that I'm not some terrible old dragon? Is it too late?"

Sara squeezed her cousin's hand. "It's never too late, Pigeon."

Pigeon gave a quick sob of relief. She grabbed Sara and held her in a warm, affectionate hug. Even Hetty King, standing in the doorway, was moved—although she would never admit it— and reached for her handkerchief to dash a few tears from her own eyes.

Pigeon held Sara at arm's length. Her eyes twinkled with merriment. "Shall we try to fix things?" she asked.

Sara nodded with glee, smiling widely now.

"Well, bear with me." She winked. "I have a plan."

"Mr. Frewen," Pigeon called, tapping the barn door with her umbrella. "If you don't mind, may I have a word with you?"

Sara and Pigeon entered the barn. Pat regarded them suspiciously.

"I don't want to talk to her, Sara," he said with a snort before turning his attention back to his sow.

"Mr. Frewen, I know how you feel, but

please, for Theodora's sake, just listen," Sara pleaded.

Pat dumped a bucket of slop in the trough. He took his time before letting on that he might be ready to listen. Crossing his hands on his chest, he faced them, but he didn't budge an inch.

Pigeon approached him, stepping gingerly over to the pig sty. "Please, Mr. Frewen, let me apologize. I was abominably rude and insensitive to the miscommunication we were both under, and I'm so dreadfully sorry about it."

"You are?" Pat asked skeptically.

"From the bottom of my heart, I am. I'm really so sorry, I could just die. I feel so badly about it."

Pat gave a curt nod. The apology was sufficient.

"With your permission," Pigeon continued, "I would like very much to help you win back the love of your dear Theodora."

"Forget it, it's a lost cause," he said gruffly. "She don't want me."

"Please, talk to her just one more time," Sara pleaded.

Pat remained dubious. "What do you reckon I should do?" he asked.

That was just the invitation they needed. With an eager excitement, the two conspirators described their plan.

Chapter Twenty

Almost a hundred people showed up to hear Pigeon Plumtree and Sara Stanley recite for the Improvement Society. Sara looked from behind the curtain at the murmuring sea of faces. Her stomach danced with excitement. Never before had she performed in front of so many people.

Pigeon winked at her. As if she could read Sara's mind, she whispered, "Any actress worth her salt experiences stage fright." Sara smiled with relief.

Meanwhile, at the doorway, a small commotion broke out as Felicity tugged and pushed, coaxed and cajoled in a vain attempt to get Theodora Dixon through the door.

"I came to support the Improvement Society, but under the circumstances, I don't think that I want to set foot in the same room as that woman," Theodora insisted, firmly clutching the doorframe.

Felicity tried one more ploy. "Now, Miss

Dixon, you know how people will talk. You don't want them to think that you're jealous of Miss Plumtree, do you?"

"Jealous? I'm not jealous," Theodora asserted, even though she was. Still, rather than let the gossips of Avonlea think that Pigeon Plumtree had got the better of her, Theodora straightened her hat, smoothed her hair and, with as much grace as she could muster, took a seat in the audience. The members of the planning committee smiled at her in sympathy, admiring her courage.

There was a call for quiet. Sara and Pigeon stepped onto the little platform stage that had been built especially for the occasion. All the rustling and murmuring quickly settled down and an expectant hush fell over the room.

Pigeon nodded to Sara to start her piece. Sara swallowed hard. Pigeon smiled her encouragement and gave a slight wink.

Sara took one step forward. Clasping her hands in front of her, as she had been instructed to do, she began: "'You know we French stormed Ratisbonne ...'"

Once she had begun, she forgot her nerves, so caught up was she in the tale. The audience disappeared, and in their place Sara conjured for herself and for those who listened an image of Napoleon in his camp, and the brave boy who brought him news of victory.

Sara enthralled her audience, making her teacher proud. As Pigeon had taught her, Sara made her voice grave and deep when speaking as Napoleon, light and innocent when playing the boy. When she came to the last line—"'And smiling, the boy fell dead'"—there wasn't a person there who didn't feel a lump in their throat.

The audience thundered its applause. Sara took several bows. She surveyed the audience and saw Aunt Hetty clapping louder than the rest.

Next it was Pigeon's turn. Avonlea now had its chance to see true artistry. All the great heroines were paraded on that little stage that night: the evil Lady Macbeth, the mad Ophelia, the royal Cleopatra. Pigeon's magnificent voice, her flawless interpretation, the intensity of her passion aroused a grand passion in her audience.

But it was her tragic Juliet that made the biggest impression on her audience and would live longest in their memories. When Pigeon lifted the dagger and charged, "'This is thy sheath; there rest, and let me die,'" plunging the bitter point into her innocent heart, there was no one there who didn't believe, just for a moment, that she had actually died.

It was a magnificent program, everyone agreed. Pigeon bowed graciously to the applause. Then, after her fifth bow, she gestured for silence. She motioned to Sara to come and join her.

"Thank you, thank you, one and all. On behalf of my cousin, Sara Stanley, and myself, I wish to make a personal donation." Pigeon scanned the audience. "Miss Theodora Dixon, are you here? As treasurer of the Avonlea Village Improvement Society, would you kindly step to the stage to accept this small token of my support for your worthy organization?"

Theodora slumped down in her chair, vigorously shaking her head, but a reproving glance from Hetty King proved strong encouragement. Collecting her composure, Theodora made it, somehow, to the stage.

Theodora's feelings against Pigeon were still so strong that she could barely look at the woman. With her head averted, she gingerly accepted the cheque Pigeon held out to her.

After a couple of tries, Theodora finally found her voice and managed to say, with very little enthusiasm, "On behalf of the Avonlea Village Improvement Society, I would like to extend my heartiest thanks for your ..."

Theodora looked at the cheque. It was a lavish amount—far more than she might have expected. Theodora's eyes nearly popped out of her head when she saw that Pigeon had donated a hundred dollars! She could barely contain her excitement as she concluded, "... your generous gift!"

The audience once again broke into applause. Theodora started from the stage.

"Not so fast, my dear," Pigeon whispered, catching Theodora by the sleeve and pulling her back beside her. "Ladies and gentleman, just one final word." Pigeon paused until she was sure she had the attention of everyone present. "While the people in the community thought that I was coaching Sara Stanley, my talented protégée, how to act, in truth, I was also coaching someone else in a matter of the heart."

Theodora stood in a state of confusion. Whatever was this woman talking about? Her bewilderment increased tenfold when Pat Frewen, decked out in his Sunday best, walked on the stage. Whispers rustled through the audience.

Pigeon was the only one unruffled. "I was helping a very nice man who wanted to learn the correct way of speaking to the woman he loves," she continued.

Theodora turned and would have hightailed it from the stage if Pigeon had not grabbed her arm and held her close beside her.

Pat hesitated for a minute. Sara had to encourage him with a little shove. Gathering all his courage, Pat approached his lady love. Suddenly, he dropped to his knee.

"Theodora," he declared, "I ain't much, and I know I made a fool of myself, but I love you and I wish you'd be my wife. And let's just get this thing over with," he added somewhat desperately, hoping to get out of the public eye as fast as possible.

"Oh for heaven's sake, get up off your knees," Theodora scolded, outwardly annoyed but privately pleased. "Donate ten dollars to the Improvement Society and I will say yes."

"Make it five," Pat bargained.

"Ten, or I will say no." Theodora remained firm.

Pat reached into his pocket and pulled out a bill. With a sigh of resignation he capitulated. "You drive a hard bargain, but you're worth it. Ten it is."

The audience burst into thunderous applause. To everyone's great relief, the longest running drama in Avonlea had ended happily after all.

Shortly after the performance, Pigeon left Avonlea. She had enjoyed her holiday, but the lure of the stage was too great for her to resist.

Before she departed, she stopped by Rose Cottage and spent a pleasant afternoon with Sara and Hetty King, who was now one of her biggest fans.

"Can I offer you some cake before you go?" Hetty asked her guest.

"Darling, you know I simply can't have sweets when I'm about to travel—think of the indigestion!"

"Oh come now. Just a smidgen, Pigeon?" Hetty urged. "Oh! My! That was a rhyme, wasn't it?"

"Aunt Hetty, we'll make an actress of you after all," said Sara, "won't we, Pigeon?"

"Adieu, dear heart, I shall miss you." Pigeon embraced Sara one last time.

"We shall never forget you, Pigeon. Will we, Aunt Hetty?"

"How could we forget?" Hetty asked, uncharitably remembering the Belgium chocolates.

And so, after more fond farewells, Pigeon flew from Sara's life.

The next weekend, Pat Frewen finally married Theodora Dixon. The whole town turned out for the event they had waited so long to see.

Some thought that the wedding was a bit rushed, as Pat had only just proposed a few days earlier. But, as others pointed out, if you added up the all those long years, it didn't seem hasty at all.

Sara and Felicity walked up the aisle as bridesmaids. Pat Frewen, decked out in his brand new suit, stood proudly at the altar. Everyone agreed that they had never seen Theodora look as radiant as she did when she marched to meet the man she had loved, and loved loyally, for twenty years.

❦   ❦   ❦